P9-DGU-869

Hunter's Big Sister

By Laura Malone Elliott

Illustrations by Lynn Munsinger

KATHERINE TEGEN BOOKS

An Imprint of HarperCollinsPublishers

Also Available
HUNTER'S BEST FRIEND AT SCHOOL
HUNTER & STRIPE AND THE SOCCER SHOWDOWN

Hunter's Big Sister
Text copyright © 2007 by Laura Malone Elliott
Illustrations copyright © 2007 by Lynn Munsinger

Manufactured in China.
All rights reserved. No part of this book may be used or reproduced in
any manner whatsoever without written permission except in the case of
brief quotations embodied in critical articles and reviews. For information
address HarperCollins Children's Books, a division of HarperCollins
Publishers, 1350 Avenue of the Americas, New York, NY 10019.
www.harpercollinschildrens.com
Library of Congress Cataloging-in-Publication Data is available.
ISBN-10: 0-06-000233-6 — ISBN-13: 978-0-06-000233-6
ISBN-10: 0-06-000234-4 (lib. bdg.) — ISBN-13: 978-0-06-000234-3 (lib. bdg.)
Typography by Jeanne L. Hogle   1 2 3 4 5 6 7 8 9 10   ❖   First Edition

To Megan and Peter
—L.M.E.

To Hailey, Alexia, and Izabel
—L.M.

Glenna was Hunter's big sister. She was very smart. She knew the names of all the bones in a raccoon's body and the capitals of twenty countries. She could even multiply six by eight and get it right.

But, best of all, she knew every fairy tale. She'd act them out with Hunter. Glenna decided who they'd play.

In *Sleeping Beauty,*
Glenna was the princess,

the good fairies,

and the prince.

Hunter got to be the hedge of roses.

In *Cinderaccoon,* Glenna
played Cinderaccoon,

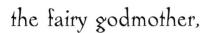

the fairy godmother,

and Prince Charming.

Hunter was the pumpkin
that turned into a coach.

In *The Princess and the Pea,* Glenna was, of course, the beautiful maiden. Hunter was the pea.

Hunter loved Glenna very much. He didn't care that she was bossy—well, most of the time—as long as she played with him. When she had other things to do, he couldn't help pestering her to get her attention. Besides, it was so much fun.

When she was outside on the swing set with her friends,
Hunter made faces out the window or waved the valentine
that Rob, the raccoon next door, had sent her.

When Glenna did math homework, Hunter would creep up behind her and tie signs to her tail.

When Glenna practiced Mozart sonatas, Hunter boogie-danced. If she ignored him, he'd sing as loudly as possible: "Blama-rama-ding-dong, doo-wop, doo-wop."

But what Glenna hated most of all was when Hunter copied her. He was an excellent mimic. He could sound just like her.

"Hunter, that's *really* annoying," Glenna would say.

Hunter would grin and parrot: "Hunter, that's *really* annoying."

"Stop it, please."

"Stop it, please."

"MOM!"

"MOM!"

That's about the time Hunter
would run away and disappear.

"He's just teasing you because he loves you," Glenna's mother told her. "He'll grow out of it soon."

"Let's hope he does tomorrow," grumbled Glenna.

But he didn't.

One day Hunter and Glenna were in their tree house
playing *Raccoonstiltskin*. Hunter was getting tired of rolling
his head around like a spinning wheel. So he started
copying Glenna.

"Alas," said Glenna, playing the miller's daughter, "I must
spin this straw into gold before dawn or die."

"Alas," repeated Hunter, "I must spin this straw into gold
before dawn or die."

Glenna frowned. "That's my line."

Hunter frowned. "That's my line."

"AAAHHHH! I'm not going to play with you anymore if you start being a copycat." Glenna stomped to the edge of the tree house.

Hunter stomped after her.

Then a really scary thing happened.

Glenna was usually an expert tree climber. All little raccoons are. But she was dressed in one of their mom's old ball gowns. She was also annoyed. She didn't notice that, as she scrambled down the tree trunk, the hem of her dress caught on a branch.

It held fast and yanked Glenna off balance.

First she scraped her knees along the tree bark. Then she swung in midair. Finally she fell, her dress fluttering behind.

THUMP.

"OOWW!" Glenna started to cry. "Hunter, go tell Mom
I'm hurt! Hurry!"

Hunter ran for the house as fast as he could. He felt terrible. Glenna had fallen because he'd been pestering her.

Hunter burst into the kitchen.

"Just a minute, sweetie," his mother muttered as she
measured cake ingredients.

Hunter was so used to mimicking Glenna, he just blurted out, "Go tell Mom I'm hurt!"

His mother was puzzled for only a moment. Darting out the door, she called, "Glenna?"

Hunter started to follow. But being the good copycat he was, he realized his mother had forgotten things he'd seen her use before—an ice pack, medicine, bandages. Hunter even grabbed a pillow for Glenna's head.

He threw everything into his red wagon and pulled it down the hill. "Hunter Ambulance to the rescue!" he called.

He propped Glenna up on the pillow and kissed her forehead. "Tell us where it hurts," he said, sounding just like his mother.

Glenna wasn't hurt badly. She needed a bandage for a scrape plus a cherry Popsicle to feel better in general.

"Did I do okay getting Mom?" Hunter asked.

"You did great."

Glenna hugged him.

"I'm sorry I was a copycat," he said.

"I'm sorry I was bossy," she said.

"Can we stop playing *Raccoonstiltskin* now?"

"Sure," said Glenna. "Let's play hospital. You're good at that."

She even let Hunter be the doctor.